Don't count the number of birthdays.
Count how happy you feel. I'm Birthday
Bear, and I'll help make your birthdays
the best ever.

I'm Wish Bear, and if
you wish on my star,
maybe your special dream
will come true.

If you're ever feeling lonely,
just call on me, Friend Bear.
See, I've got a daisy for you
and a daisy for me.

Grr! I'm Grumpy Bear. There's a cloud on
my tummy to show that I take the grouchies
away, so you can be happy again.

I'm Love-a-Lot Bear. I have two
hearts on my tummy. One is for you;
the other is for someone you love.

It's my job to bring you sweet dreams.
I'm Bedtime Bear, and right now I'm a bit
sleepy. Are you sleepy, too?

Now that you know all of us, we hope
that you'll have a special place for us in your
heart, just like we do for you.

With love from all of us,

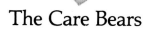

The Care Bears

Copyright © 1983 by Parker Brothers, Division of CPG Products Corp. All rights reserved.
Published in the United States by Parker Brothers, Division of CPG Products Corp.

Care Bears, Tenderheart Bear, Friend Bear, Grumpy Bear, Birthday Bear, Cheer Bear, Bedtime Bear, Funshine Bear, Love-a-Lot
Bear, Wish Bear and Good Luck Bear are trademarks of American Greetings Corporation.

Library of Congress Cataloging in Publication Data: Morgan, Stephanie. The witch down the street. SUMMARY: Three Care Bears
from the land of Care-a-lot help Melissa see that the woman she thought was a witch is just a lonely old lady.
[1. Witches—Fiction. 2. Bears—Fiction] I. Cooke, Tom, ill.
II. Title. PZ7.M82644Wi 1982 [E] 82-22329 ISBN: 0-910313-02-4
Manufactured in the United States of America.   4 5 6 7 8 9 0

A Tale from the
Care Bears™
The Witch Down the Street

Story by Stephanie Morgan
Pictures by Tom Cooke

Melissa was walking home from school when she passed old Mrs. Burke. "Why, hello there, Melissa," Mrs. Burke said. "I haven't seen you for a long time. Would you like to stop in for some cookies?"

"No! . . . I mean no thank you, Mrs. Burke." Melissa said nervously, and she quickly ran down the block.

When Melissa was younger, she used to visit Mrs. Burke, but now that she was in school the other children had told her that Mrs. Burke was a witch.

It had to be true. Last week didn't Melissa see Mrs. Burke talking to her black cat? And the other children said Mrs. Burke poisoned the apples from the tree in her backyard and gave them out on Halloween.

Melissa didn't want a witch living down the street, so she said, "Yes," when her friend Jamie dared her to play a trick on old Mrs. Burke.

On Monday afternoon Melissa tacked a large note to Mrs. Burke's door. She rang the doorbell and ran down the street to where Jamie was hiding. They looked back at Mrs. Burke's house.

Melissa saw Mrs. Burke open the door. Mrs. Burke was smiling as if she were going to meet a friend, but when she saw the note, she stopped smiling. The note read:

"Mrs. Burke is old and mean,
The ugliest witch we've ever seen."

Mrs. Burke stared at the note for a long time. Then she slowly went back inside.

Melissa knew that she was supposed to feel glad that she had played a trick on the old witch down the street, but now, somehow, the trick didn't seem so great after all.

The next day as Melissa was walking home from school, she got a surprise. Standing at the big blue mailbox on the corner, holding a large stack of envelopes, was a small Bear with two hearts on its tummy.

The Bear floated up to the mail slot, put in an envelope and floated down to the ground again, landing with a soft bump.

"What are you doing here?" Melissa asked.

"Mailing friendship notes," the Bear said happily.
"I love to have friends."

"You must know a lot of people," Melissa said.

"I know a lot of people who need friendship," said
the Bear.

"Do you live around here?" Melissa asked. "I've never seen you before."

"No, I live in Care-a-lot, the warm and snuggly home of the Care Bears. It's very nice there," said the Bear. "It's just that the mailbox I always use was filled up."

The Bear crossed the street, and Melissa, who had never seen such an unusual Bear before, followed.

"Who are you?" Melissa asked.

"I'm Love-a-Lot. I help people love each other. If love doesn't find a way, I will!"

Love-a-Lot leaned over and scooped up some snow and made it into a heart-shaped snowball. "This is for you," Love-a-Lot said to Melissa.

Then Love-a-Lot made another snow heart, and
ran up Mrs. Burke's walk, and put it on her porch.
   Melissa was startled to find that they were in front
of Mrs. Burke's house.

"Why did you do that?" Melissa said. "Don't you know who lives there?"

"Everybody needs love," Love-a-Lot replied.

"Even witches?"

"Even lonely old ladies," said Love-a-Lot gently.

"But everyone *knows* she's a witch," Melissa insisted.

"Some people *say* she's a witch." Love-a-Lot corrected.

"All the kids are afraid of her," Melissa said.

"Then Mrs. Burke must need a lot of love," replied Love-a-Lot softly. "Don't you think so?" Then Love-a-Lot made another snow heart. "For you."

"Thank you," said Melissa. "But why are you giving me another one?"

"Why keep my heart to myself?" Love-a-Lot smiled. "It makes me happier to give it to someone. Well, I'd better be going. I've got more notes to write." And the little Bear scampered away.

As Melissa walked the rest of the way to her house and up to her room, she thought about Love-a-Lot's words.

When she got to her room, she discovered another Care Bear, a little yellow one, sitting on her desk.

Melissa gasped in surprise. "Who are you?" she asked.

"I'm Birthday Bear. Love-a-Lot told all us Care Bears about you, so I came to see you," the Bear said.

Melissa was puzzled. "But my birthday isn't for two months."

"I know, but there is someone else we both know whose birthday is the day after tomorrow."

Melissa wondered whom Birthday Bear was talking about.

Birthday Bear floated off the desk. "But it's so hard to plan anything when I'm hungry." He looked at Melissa hopefully. "You wouldn't happen to have a jelly sandwich with you?"

"No, but I could make you one."

"Yes, please," said Birthday Bear. "And some soda to wash it down?"

"You'll get fat if you eat too much of this stuff," said Melissa after she had brought the food up from the kitchen.

"No I won't. The only food that is fattening is peanuts."

"How do you know?" Melissa asked.

"Did you ever see a skinny elephant?"

Birthday Bear was so pleased with his answer that he rolled on the floor and laughed and laughed. "Oh, I do love a joke," he said as he got up. "But now it's time to get to work."

Birthday Bear pointed to the cake on his tummy. "Now, birthdays should be happy, right?"

"Of course," said Melissa.

"But what about someone who hasn't had a happy birthday in a long time? She lives by herself, and . . ." Birthday Bear looked right at Melissa. ". . . sometimes people play mean tricks on her."

"You mean Mrs. Burke, don't you?" Melissa asked quietly.

"Exactly."

"But she's a witch," Melissa said, "isn't she?"

"Oh, she's no witch. She's just a lonely old lady who would like a friend. Do you know the only way she could get her broom to fly?"

"How?" Melissa asked.

"Buy it a ticket on an airplane!" Birthday Bear cried. "Get it?" And then he started to roll on the floor again. When he stopped laughing, he jumped up and said seriously, "Back to work now, back to work."

He walked over to Melissa's toy piano, sat down, and tapped out "Happy Birthday to You." "Let's sing together," he said.

Melissa closed her eyes and sang along. Suddenly she knew what to do for Mrs. Burke's birthday, and she felt good inside.

But on the day of Mrs. Burke's birthday Melissa still hadn't decided if she was brave enough to carry out her plan. She remembered what the Care Bears had said, but she was still afraid to knock on Mrs. Burke's door.

When Melissa left her house that morning, she saw *another* Care Bear standing in her front yard, rolling a big ball of snow on the ground.

"Hi there!" the Care Bear waved. The Bear had a smiling sun on its tummy. "Want to help me build a snow bear?"

"Sure," said Melissa. "But which Care Bear are you?"

"Ho! That's a good one." The Bear pointed to the smiling sun. "I'm Funshine Bear, and I try to enjoy each moment of the day. Come and help me."

"Isn't this fun?" Funshine Bear asked. "I love to build snow bears, but it's more fun with you to help. Share the fun and you get twice as much; that's what I always say."

"You must be a share bear," Melissa joked.

"Ho! That's another good one. You know, I'm *really* a Care Bear."

Melissa reached out and drew a smiling sun on the snow bear's tummy with her finger.

"How nice!" Funshine exclaimed. "I'm very flattered. You must like to share too. You know what would be really fun? A party. Don't you love parties?"

"Most of the time," Melissa said carefully.

"But what kind of party could we have?" Funshine Bear asked. Then Funshine did a little dance in the snow. "Oh, now I remember. There's somebody who needs a little fun on her birthday. Birthday Bear told me all about her. But I seem to have forgotten her name."

"Mrs. Burke?" Melissa asked quietly.

"That's it! Wouldn't it be fun to give her a good time on her birthday?"

"Well . . ." Melissa thought about Mrs. Burke all alone with only her cat for company. And on her *birthday*. "Will you go with me?" she asked.

"Yes," said Funshine Bear. "And I'll be outside watching every minute, just to make sure you are enjoying yourself."

Melissa walked slowly up the path to Mrs. Burke's door.

Funshine peered around the corner of the house and whispered, "Go on. I'll be right here. Be brave. She's going to be so surprised. I can't wait!"

Melissa took a deep breath and rang the bell.

The door opened, and Mrs. Burke looked at her suspiciously. "What do you want?" the old lady said.

Melissa was so scared that she could hardly speak, but she reached into her bag, took a deep breath and said, "H—happy birthday, Mrs. B—burke."

Mrs. Burke's mouth dropped open in surprise. "How did you know it was my birthday?"

"Someone who cares about you told me."

"What? Oh, this is wonderful." Mrs. Burke read the card. "You made it yourself. How beautiful." Mrs. Burke was smiling, but it looked as if she might cry. "Come in. Come in, and help me celebrate. I never expected—I mean, I haven't had a birthday card in years. What a thoughtful child you are."

Right then Melissa knew that her friends, the Care Bears, were right. Mrs. Burke wasn't a witch at all. A party with her would be fun. Melissa went right into Mrs. Burke's house, ate two pieces of homemade apple pie, and sang "Happy Birthday" to Mrs. Burke. While she was singing she glanced up and saw three pairs of eyes peeking through the window. The Care Bears had come to the party too!

After the party Melissa walked home and there, pinned to her front door, was a note:

"This is a friendship note to a special girl. Always remember to share your heart, and please remember us.

Your friends,
Funshine, Birthday, and
Love-a-Lot."